Martian Odyssey

Tom Riley

HERITAGE BOOKS
2018

HERITAGE BOOKS

AN IMPRINT OF HERITAGE BOOKS, INC.

Books, CDs, and more—Worldwide

For our listing of thousands of titles see our website
at
www.HeritageBooks.com

Published 2018 by
HERITAGE BOOKS, INC.
Publishing Division
5810 Ruatan Street
Berwyn Heights, Md. 20740

International Standard Book Numbers
Paperbound: 978-0-7884-5863-7

This book is dedicated to my wonderful, patient wife, Crucy, my two daughters, Dr. Gina Riley, Ph.D and Dr. Bernadette Riley, D.O and my grandson, Benjamin Noah Riley, classical guitarist.

The author would like to thank the National Aeronautics and Space Administration for the use of photos, graphs, renderings and drawings that appear in this novel.

The author was inspired to write this book when he joined the Air Force at seventeen, was trained as a photographer, and received Secret Clearance during the two years he was stationed at Edwards Air Force Base in California. Edwards was an Air Research and Development Base and was featured in the movie, *The Right Stuff.* Tom was assigned as a photographer and worked on the X-15, B-52's, B-58's, nuclear weapons, rockets and experimental aircrafts. As an Airman First Class he received Top Secret Clearance and was among the first 5000 soldiers sent to support the war in Vietnam shortly after being named Airman of the Month at Edwards Air Force Base. He was stationed at Clark Air Force Base in the Philippines. The author served in the Air Force from 1959–1963. He later attended LIU and Iona College on the G.I. Bill.

Tom Riley is the author of ten books and over 2,500 articles written for newspapers and magazines. You can find a list of his books on his website:
theorphantrainriders.com and at heritagebooks.com.

CHAPTER I

The Doomsday clock had finally struck. North Korea made a pre-emptive strike against Japan, South Korea and the West Coast of the United States and many of the truck-borne missiles were on their way to Guam, site of a massive American arsenal of bombers, fighter jets and nuclear weapons. The Americans had been aware of the pre-emptive strike and intercepted many of the missiles but a few had gotten through the defensive Patriot Missile Batteries and caused massive casualties in Japan and South Korea.

Kim Ill Jung, at the end of his rope, had caused a massive collapse of a mountain housing his main nuclear testing station complex. Not satisfied with producing over one hundred atomic bombs he had decided he wanted to develop a mini hydrogen bomb and test it at the complex housing over 1,000 men and women, causing their demise. The test was against the advice of his scientists. The growing rebellion against his rule made it imperative he assert his control over his generals — his single-minded focus to be the *Dr. No of the world* drove him to madness.

It was the last year of President Thyson's presidency and he asked world leaders for restraint; China had invaded North Korea amid terrible spreading radiation from targeted U.S. strikes against Kim Ill Jung's arsenal of nuclear weapons and many Chinese troops were dying of radiation. Kim Ill Jung was found in a cave and torn apart by peasants seeking shelter. Russia too was alarmed at the amount of radiation spreading into Russian territory. India and Pakistan were threatening to settle old scores. It was during these perilous times that President Thyson authorized the *Courage One* Mission to Mars in the hope of inspiring humankind away from war and toward peaceful exploration of space.

President Thyson had fought for funding for the Variable Specific Magnetoplasma Rocket Engine because it could propel humans to Mars in thirty-nine days instead of the prevailing nine month voyage. NASA had selected the Texas based Nova Rocket Company and former astronaut, Dr. Franklin Diaz Chang's design because time was of a necessity and world affairs were at a razor's edge with rising rhetoric and inflammatory threats from nations who had historical differences spanning centuries.

Courtesy of NASA website.

Commander Michael Ryan, a veteran of two trips to the moon knew the importance of the mission. He and the four other astronauts had been working together for a year as the VASIMR rocket had been perfected. They were anxious to work inside the real rocket but had to work inside a module as the scientists worked to eliminate the bugs in the plasma rocket and the nuclear engine that would carry them home.

Colonel Michael Ryan on his second trip to the moon.

Rendering courtesy of NASA website.

The former Air Force colonel and jet fighter pilot felt fortunate to have been chosen mission commander and reflected on his life. When he was seven his mother died and he and his brothers and sisters were shipped off to a children's home, since his father had abandoned the family years earlier. After graduating high school he immediately joined the Air Force. After two years he rose to the rank of sergeant and took a test for Officer's Training School. He was sent to the Air Force Academy and passed numerous tests to become a fighter pilot. He shot down four Syrian jets in three days after the Syrian government launched a chemical attack against the rebels killing children, women and men en masse. Two years later he was invited by NASA to join their space program. Little did he think he would be leading the free world in an attempt to find another home for mankind should we make our planet uninhabitable because of a nuclear war.

The VASIMR plasma rocket heads to Mars with five astronauts aboard in an attempt to land on mars.

From leading a fighter squadron in Afghanistan to being chosen for the Astronaut Corps ten years ago had been a long and difficult journey. He knew one thing: teamwork, perseverance and the ability to withstand pain had made him a leader. The foundation laid by the Air Force Academy, aerospace training, the Moon trips and thousands of hours in the space station had prepared him for command. He had been aboard when two payload re-supply rockets imploded at the launch site.

After waiting two extra months, a Russian re-supply ship finally delivered much needed supplies. Each astronaut had lost between ten and fifteen pounds.

The experience had taught him NASA's training to prepare for every emergency and the importance of redundant systems, creativity and improvising could get you through almost every failure or breakdown in equipment. The command of men and women during emergencies had brought Michael's leadership qualities to the forefront and the administration at NASA knew they had the right man to lead the Mars Mission.

The infighting to be the commander of the first human settlement of Mars was fierce though no one spoke of it. There was a silent acknowledgement that every day they would be tested and graded and the determination would be made weeks before the end of their training. The astronauts, scientists, physicians, generals and test pilots who were their mentors would compare notes and determine who had the right stuff to be made commander of *Courage One*. Failure of the mission was never an option. The need to find humankind another place to live was an absolute necessity.

Chapter II

For the last seven years robots and 3-D printers had been building a small habitable village for the first Mars landing of astronauts. The Dome built by 3-D printers inside a crater on Mt. Sharp provided housing and labs so that the astronauts could remove their hard suits and work in comfort. They had found a permanent source of water near the landing base and had increased the oxygen level in the Domes by seven percent by planting beds of Earth bacteria and seedlings that can survive the low pressure conditions found on Mars. Researcher had found Serratia Liquefaciens can survive the harsh conditions, low oxygen and freezing temperature. This along with Carnobacterium, a hardy bacteria, were surprisingly adaptive to Mars' cold and carbon dioxide-rich atmosphere. Ultraviolet shielding was enabling the bacteria to survive.

Outside the Dome, robots and rovers were terraforming a mile square of the Martian surface with the bacteria and seedlings and shielding them with an ultraviolet film. The constant sandstorms initially destroyed these outdoor greenhouses but improvements had been made to curtail the damage and the effort was expanding. *Courage One* was to add 150 rovers, seedlings and bacteria, hardy trees and bushes in an effort to speed up the process.

By using solar mirrors focused on the crater at Mt. Sharp they were able to increase the ambient temperature by twenty-five degrees. The permanent source of water created a small lake and park under one of the domes. A small ozone layer was created. The planned mission was for ninety days and the five astronauts updated the base with newly discovered hyper-oxygen bearing plants and bushes.

Rockets were sent on nine-month trips filled with huge 3-D printers that built multi-level buildings that could withstand sandstorms. These 3-D printers were able to include electrical systems and plumbing which would be activated once the astronauts arrived and hooked it up with the nuclear rocket. This boon to accommodating life on Mars convinced President Trump to go ahead with a mission that would keep Earth-bound residents spellbound during perilous times. Should the thirty-nine day trip to Mars succeed, many more missions were planned.

Eventually a small city would be established on Mt. Sharp. The printers would be able to manufacture anything that was needed by the residents of the city, from simple utensils to motors, drones, gliders and any material needs for Martian habitation. They would use elements found in Martian geology as building material. These same printers would build greenhouses, hospitals, warehouses and more. All medical equipment would be manufactured by the printers. Should trauma or wounds occur among the inhabitants of Mars, the printers would treat the wounds with human tissue and skin on-site until they could receive care in a hospital. The limits to the use of 3-D printers for all kinds of projects was only limited by the imagination of mankind.

Ryan always loved William Faulkner, the great southern; especially the novelist's reaffirmation of humanity when he said, "I decline to accept the end of man. I believe Man will not only merely endure, he will prevail. He is immortal not because he alone among creatures has an inexhaustible voice, but because he has a soul, a spirit capable of compassion and sacrifice and endurance. The poet's duty is to write about these things. It is his privilege to help man endure by lifting his heart, by reminding him of the courage and honor and hope and pride and compassion and pity and sacrifice which have been the glory of his past. The poet's voice need not merely be the record of man, it can be one of the props, the pillars to help him endure and prevail."

Mars before *Courage One*'s arrival.

Photo courtesy of NASA website.

NASA's rendering of a futuristic Martian city.

The First Martian City on the Red Planet is constructed by computers and 3-D printers utilizing Martian geology and materials gathered from the Martian surface.

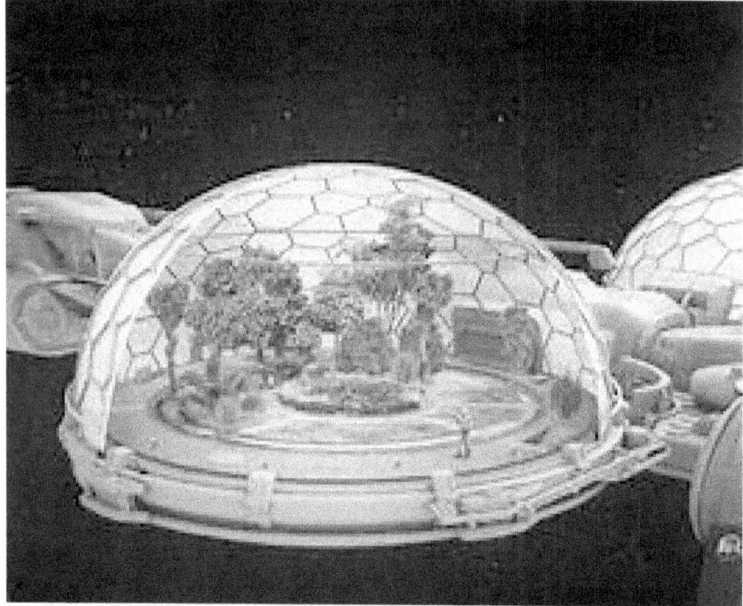

Rendering courtesy of NASA website.

CHAPTER III

On the 38th Day

David Chang, flight engineer and first mate, handed Ryan a cup of Java. "We're getting close to touchdown Commander. The Vasimr engine and nuclear rocket are working smoothly. Heating is being adjusted as freezing temperatures are being adjusted hourly. We experienced a bit of space junk. A lot more countries have tried to reach Mars than we previously thought. We've accelerated past the larger chunks and the rest ricochets off the rocket skin."

"That's the racket I heard last night," said Ryan as he sat back and gently massaged his eyelids trying to stay awake. He had been at the helm of *Courage One* for sixteen hours and he felt a dire need for sleep. "What's the damage? Start with the bad news first; let's hear it."

"The water tank is ruptured and there are dents all over the exterior module. We've repaired the leak but not before losing 200 gallons of water. Luckily everything electrically is working and the landing module seems to have withstood all the buffeting but we may not know for sure until we try and stick the landing. The oxygen generators and bacterial units are good, all personnel are safe, a few solar panels are shattered and the experimental lab is in disarray, but it's nothing we can't fix once we've landed," said Chang.

"What about the 3-D printers, robots and rovers? We'll need them soon. In twenty-four hours we'll be touching down," said Ryan.

"Everything is locked down and ready for use," said Chang. "Bluford is doing a manual spacewalk to check the skin shield and the solar arrays."

"Damn space debris... never thought after more than a month in space, it's human junk that could do us in. Mostly Chinese and Russia stuff. Hope there are no targeting weapons in this space junkyard. China has been claiming to have developed a space laser capable of picking off enemy spaceships. They can't make it to the Red Planet but they would love to destroy an American effort at aiding mankind," said Ryan.

"Get some sleep, Commander. You're going to need it tomorrow. It's going to be the biggest day in all our lives. "

Ryan and Chang's proposed landing on Mars.

Rendering courtesy of NASA website.

Courage One positioning for the first landing on Mars by mankind.

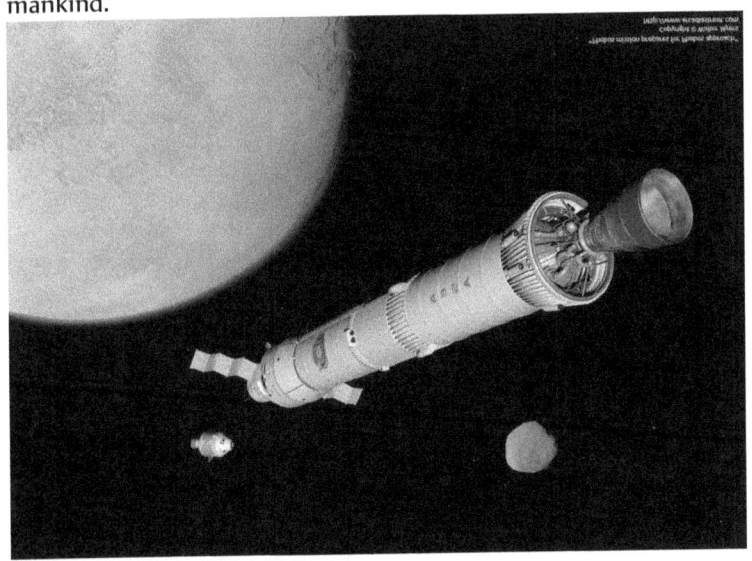

All hands were on the space deck, excitedly preparing for man's first landing on Mars. Navigation and communications director, James Bluford had completed a spacewalk and pronounced that *Courage One* had withstood a barrage of debris and was remarkably unscathed and all systems were go. "No debris has penetrated the skin and navigation GPS has us positioned to land on Mt. Sharp in four hours. There is a little concern about a sandstorm on Mt. Sharp, but hopefully it will end soon."

Space Colonization Specialist and Education Director Ann Maria Dante said, "We had to do a little housekeeping during abrupt changes while avoiding large debris but everything is in order in the lab. Astronaut health is fine and our fitness equipment has been used daily to overcome bone loss. The plants for food and growing on Mars are flourishing. The potatoes, beans and vegetables are growing faster than expected. And we have lots of fertilizer to neutralize the toxic Martian soil. By analyzing the Martian soil make-up we've developed a great potting mix that blocks ultraviolet rays."

A planned greenhouse module on Mars.

Astronaut and Transportation Specialist Marta Diaz brought coffee and bagels into the crew quarters and passed them around to the crew. "All vehicles, rovers and robots are secured and locked for landing. The next meal is going to be on Mars barring any disasters. The nuclear generator for charging all our vehicles and rovers is hooked up and ready for operation. Although we've lost 200 gallons of water our hydrogen generator will make up for that loss in two days," said Diaz.

CHAPTER IV

Courage One has landed, successfully transporting the first humans to touch the surface of Mars.

All across the world, and especially in the United States, there was absolute joy and celebration over America's triumph and courage in perilous times. World headlines, which were filled with despair and desperation for more than a month, were now singing the praises of President Thyson and his nation's triumph in space. Every television set in the world was glued to the rocket's landing on Mars and the post-celebration by the astronauts. A camera atop the rocket beamed in pictures of the surrounding terrain at varying distances on a non-stop basis. The unloading of equipment and the astronaut's joy at being Mars-bound was a wonderful distraction for Earth-bound residents worried about their own health and safety.

Over fifteen tons of equipment had to be moved from the *mother ship* and anchored onto the Martian soil.

Generators were hooked up to the nuclear powered rocket engine to feed electricity to the charging units, labs, rovers and assorted equipment. The sandstorm had died down an hour before they landed and each astronaut consulted their individualized to-do list and the workload was heavy.

American ingenuity is responsible for mankind's first Martian landing on another planet.

Courtesy of NASA website.

The *Courage One* crew begins the 3-D printing construction of a Martian city to be completed by future voyages.

Courtesy of NASA website.

The 3-D printer-made buildings, greenhouses and laboratories were hooked up to the nuclear reactor and five houses were fully charged for the first time since they were built. A pleasant, seventy-degree temperature replaced the previously frigid air and oxygen was circulating throughout the buildings. The astronauts were looking forward to shedding their spacesuits and working in a more human environment.

"Jim, tomorrow you and Anna have to set up an emergency bunker in that cave a mile and a half from here just in case we have to leave our little village. The Astro Cart GPS is set up to take you there. We know it can protect us from ultraviolet exposure and any hurricane-force sandstorm. Images estimate it is at least 800 feet, maybe more, in depth. It'll give us a good chance to test our communication on the ground. We'll load up all the gear you'll need for the bunker, hopefully we'll never have to use it."

"We don't know what's in that cave. There could be a lava tube extending for miles. It would be a great place to research if there are microbes, water, ice or even remnants of a civilization that was forced to seek shelter from the sandstorms and ultraviolet rays. I'm looking forward to exploring it," said Jim.

"The lava tubes in Hawaii can run for miles. I suggest we limit our search the first time to a thousand yards in case of crumbling walls damaging our suits. It may also have offshoot tubes and we don't know how our radios will work to stay in contact with base," said Anna.

Astronauts James Bluford and Anna Dante explore a lava tube on Mars.

"This lava tube is amazing; it has so many off-shoots. Now we know we have a big job before us as the complexity of the underground terrain on Mars is more challenging than we thought," said Dante.

"It's as if flowing water caused all these off-shoots. If that is true then life must follow. I hope we find evidence of it," said Bluford. "We go another two hundred yards, then we'll return to base."

"Communication is starting to die; we have to get back to base," said Anna. "Just give me five more minutes. I see a blue haze coming out of one of the off-shoots." Bluford climbed over a few boulders and entered the off-shoot. "Anna!" he screamed.

"You won't believe this — an ice lagoon! Anna ran up to him, took a look, gasped and high fived Bluford. "Water on Mars, frozen in ice, just what we hope to find and we found it on our second day here. The implications of this discovery mean there must have been some living organisms around. What other great discoveries await us? We have to tell base but the signal is too weak. Let's go back. Commander Ryan will want to go deeper into the cave and take tests. Let's head back," said Anna.

Astronauts Bluford and Dante head back to base after finding an ice cave.

Underground ice melts into water.

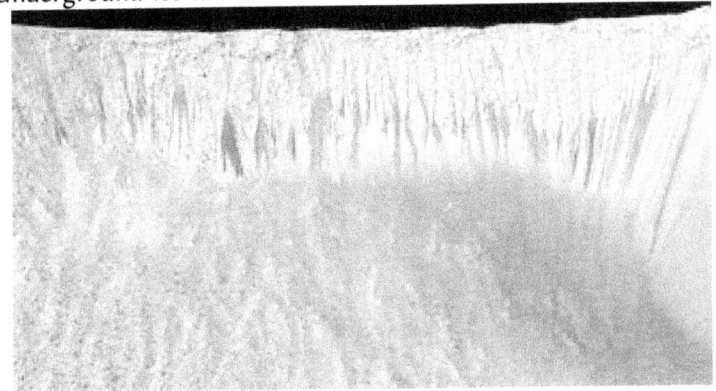

Water melts and forms in pools.

In some areas, geysers vent steam.

Fresh water is found on Mars and the astronauts know Mars can be terraformed.

CHAPTER V

The *Courage One* crew explores the ice cave.

"This is amazing — melted ice water. All the water over the ages went into the lava tubes. We can start terraforming Mars faster than we ever thought possible. The freezing surface temperatures created the ice and volcanic activity below melted it. The formations are so beautiful. The cave so far looks very stable. Bluford and Dante, do you want to take the inflatable boat and check it out for a half mile or should we go back to base and create a 3-D boat that will take us all?" asked Ryan.

"Anna, what do you say?" asked Bluford.

Anna gave a thumbs-up. They prepared the inflatable and took along Dixie GPS, a computerized dog with a cabinet of tools and items they might need. "We'll be back in forty-five minutes; if not, wait an hour. If you don't hear from us, we're in trouble or lost.

"Take good video and be safe," said Chang, "we'll take test samples and borings while you are in there."

"And we'll also do depth findings of this underground river, I wonder how far it goes and how deep it is," said Ryan.

Dante and Bluford started the five-horsepower electric motor and followed the underground river. They marveled at the abstract ice formations they passed. After fifteen minutes they stopped at an embankment and trudged through the ice cave.

"Let's stay on the main passage, there are so many offshoots we don't want to get lost," said Dante.

"Whoa, what's that up a head? It looks like a massive ice cavern!" said Bluford. They entered a huge cavern, the size of a football stadium. On the walls they could see fluctuations in the ice and water levels of the cavern. Bluford chipped off a sample and placed it in Dixie's refrigerated cabinet for storage. Bluford continued checking the ice wall for any markings or embedded material hoping to find any sign of life, microbial or otherwise. As he took multiple photos of the cavern," he said, "You could erect a small city in this cavern or a NASA Mars base, safe from the ultraviolet rays and fierce sandstorm," said Bluford.

"Jim, it's time we head back. There is always tomorrow and I'm sure there are a lot of other surprises that await us," said Anna.

They backtracked and headed toward their inflatable outboard. Dixie followed obediently barking out the distance as they sighted the boat. He leaped onboard. As they cruised along the passageway they marveled at the beauty of this icy underworld and all the surprises it held. Before long they were in sight of their comrades and excitedly told them of their discovery.

"NASA is going to be happy to hear about this. It makes their dream of terraforming Mars that much easier. By taking the oxygen molecules out of the water we can create an atmosphere for life someday," said Chang.

"I'm interested in what's in these ice chippings and what the corings tell us. Could there be microbial life embedded in the ice?" asked Ryan.

They reached the entrance to the cave and entered their space cart. In the distance they could see a sandstorm entering the horizon. "We have to get back to base real soon. That looks like a monster of a storm approaching," said Marta.

Fierce duststorm on Mars. *Courage One* races to base before the worst of the dust storm strands them in Martian sand.

Rendering courtesy of NASA website.

Martian dust storm.

Courtesy of NASA website.

"Look what's coming at us! A dust storm of apocalyptical proportions! I'm going behind that mound of rocks. I hope the *mother ship* can stand upright with these winds. We've seen these things on satellite images; to see them up close is terrifying," said Marta.

"We'll stay here until it passes. Meanwhile Chang you can upload those videos and stills to NASA on the discovery of vast amounts of water locked in ice caverns," said Ryan.

The wind and dust pounded the space cart and covered the windows with a blanket of sand. The winds were calculated to be about 125 miles per hour. A constant beeping from the *mother ship* indicated the rocket ship was undergoing tremendous vertical stress from the dust storm.

"We are in deep trouble if the ship topples over. Good thing we re-enforced the launchpad struts, fearing the speed and destructive power of these storms should they arise. Well, we know the ship is taking a battering now," said Ryan.

The group pondered inwardly the catastrophic implications of the rocket toppling over. The winds slowly subsided and the astronauts emerged from the space cart and checked their surrounding. The dust storm had dumped a foot of sand on the cart but there was no outward damage. In the distance they could see the *mother ship* still standing and gave a sigh of relief.

"Everybody back in. Let's check the base camp," said Ryan.

"The first thing we check is the green house; that place was the most vulnerable to damage," said Ryan.

Terraforming Mars.

Rendering courtesy of NASA website.

"Everything is good," reported Chang, "I've even picked some cherry tomatoes. We'll have them with pasta and meatballs tonight. I'm going to check the other out-buildings for damage. "

Chang and Bluford got in the space cart and inspected all the buildings in the base camp. Miraculously, none had been detached from their foundation or penetrated by flying rocks. They decided to check the *mother ship* to see if it had been damaged in any way. The storm had left sand drifts several feet high around the foundations of the building but the rocket ship was eight feet off the ground and with close inspection had been unaffected by the fierce winds.

"Let's head back and give a full report on the ice cave and all the water we found. I'm sure the scientists at NASA are having a field day with our initial reports. We have some ultraviolet-resistant plants that could conceivably germinate on the surface within the eighty-eight days we have left here," said Bluford.

Bluford and Chang check the outer buildings for damage.

Rendering courtesy of NASA website.

In the future, after water is pumped from the ice caves, special ultraviolet-resistant plants will be cultivated on the Martian surface in the millions to release oxygen in the atmosphere.

Ryan ponders the ultraviolet-resistant greenery he planted.

Courtesy of NASA website.

CHAPTER VI

Chang prepared a sumptuous meal of eggplant parmigiana with ziti and spaghetti and meatballs with linguini. He brought a celebratory bottle of Zinfadel for their discovery of water. "We got to get that water to the surface. We have the pumps and I've started the 3-D printers extruding hoses to channel the water toward base. Tomorrow we'll have at least a mile of hose made," said Bluford, an African American born in Washington, D.C., and a veteran of seven NASA missions. "Once I hook it up to the pumps, we'll have a permanent source of water."

"We got to unpack a lot of solar arrays and material for the printers. We have to find sources of metal and new resources on the surface that the printers could use for manufacturing. Using fusion we can crack the oxygen molecules and release them into the atmosphere. We still have a lot of exploring to do on the list NASA gave us; they want it all checked out. Bluford and Dante, I want you both to work on getting that water to base. Chang and I will get working on that to-do list; and Marta, I want you to stay at base in case we need an emergency vehicle. Check all our base operating systems and keep NASA updated," said Commander Ryan.

After dinner the crew unloaded a lot of equipment and opted to set it up in the morning. Ryan and Chang unloaded their all-terrain vehicle and loaded it with equipment they might need. They placed Dixie GPS in the vehicle. NASA wanted them to explore a canyon with unusual formations and coloring. They detected large amounts of iron and magnetism emanating from the area. The canyon was called Diablo Canyon by NASA because of its deep red coloring. It was located three miles away from base in rough terrain. They would begin the trek first thing in the morning.

Astronauts unload equipment from *Courage One.*

Rendering courtesy of NASA website.

Ryan and Chang enter Diablo Canyon.

Rendering courtesy of NASA website.

The terrain on Mars is more varied that I thought. Look at these spires. We need GPS more than ever. I would hate to get lost in this place, it's like a maze," said Chang.

"There certainly is a lot of iron in here; the magnetometer is showing greater intensity the further in we travel. At least we have a source for mining iron."

"What the hell is that up ahead. They look like cave openings built into pods. They're symmetrical so we know they're not natural," said Chang. His excitement grew at the first sign of possible life on Mars.

"This is really interesting," said Ryan. "The openings look metallic, like you would find in a bank vault. They seem to be manmade. We'd better take a weapon along just in case."

They both got out of the space cart wondering what was behind the metallic doors. They had uncovered the first sign of life on an alien planet, perhaps fulfilling man's long time desire to contact extraterrestrial beings. What was the purpose behind building these strange pods? They certainly blended in with the surroundings, making them undetectable from flyovers. They tried turning the wheel on the door but it was locked into position. There were no tracks in the Martian soil showing any recent activity. Chang and Ryan walked around the pod. It seems to be a blend of Martian soil and some composites that made it extremely hard and durable.

Ryan walks away from the Martian pod failing to open it.

Rendering courtesy of NASA website.

"I think I know what these are; they're exits and entrances to the lava tubes. They were built here in this valley because the rocky spires kept sand from burying them during dust storms," said Chang. "If we could only open them; I wonder what we'd find below? We could blow the door off, but that would signal hostile intent that definitely would backfire if we run into any Martians." Besides, NASA instructed us not to use explosives unless it was an absolutely imperative situation. Let's see if we can find another pod."

They got back into the all-terrain vehicle, passed a number of pods and went another mile before they came to a crevice in the ground.

"It looks like they started digging here but gave up for some reason. Let's grab a couple of shovels and see if we could find an entrance," said Ryan.

After twenty minutes Chang saw Martian soil pouring in a hole before his feet. Both Chang and Ryan rushed up for firmer footing. "I think we've hit upon an opening into a lava tube," said Chang. After the pouring sand subsided, Chang poked his head into the opening and waved his flashlight. "You'll never believe this Mike. There's a large room carved out of stone. I'll get the rope ladder because it's a good twenty feet to the floor."

Chang opens a passage into a room with ventilation.

Ryan and Chang enter an archway chamber room that seemed to be used for sleeping or dining by its inhabitants.

Ryan and Chang anchored the rope ladder and went into the small opening, sand pouring in as they climbed down. Their powerful searchlight lit up a room about fifty feet in circumference. In the middle of the room was a large grate where ventilation coming through signified there was at least one floor below. "I can't believe this, some kind of human-like being carved this room out of the lava. I see an opening at the far end. There are no objects laying around, why?" he asked as they made for the opening at the far end.

They entered another large room that had a passageway and two-foot high shelves running the length of it. It was more finely constructed with stone arches every eight feet running the length of the room. Again no objects were found and at the far end was an oval opening apparently leading further into the tube.

"What could this have been? Sleeping quarters or a dining area or some kind of a space for worship? Let's check out one more area and then we better head back to base," said Chang.

Chang and Ryan happen upon a cavern as big as a stadium.

They went through the passageway and gasped in disbelief. Before them was the biggest cavern they had ever seen. "I guess when they broke through the wall to expand their rooms they realized it wasn't possible to go horizontal. That vent tells me they went vertical, let's take that path, we should come to another floor soon," said Ryan. As they walked down the path they could hear water falling into the lake below. On their left they saw another room. It led into a corridor that was held up by carved stone columns. At the end of the corridor they entered a room that at first glance seemed to be a burial chamber. In the center was a sarcophagus.

They lifted the lid off the sarcophagus and were amazed at the find. Inside was an elongated humanoid skull. "Our first Martian discovery; we now know Mars was inhabited. Maybe this was a Martian king, given his own private burial chamber. Why so bare though and no drawings or writings telling us who she or he was, and just the skull, no skeletal remains," said Chang.

Ryan looked closely at the skull and the inside of the burial chamber but there was nothing visible, just an elongated skull. He had always been fascinated by Egyptian archeology and knew this ritual was revered by the ruling class and the pharaohs.

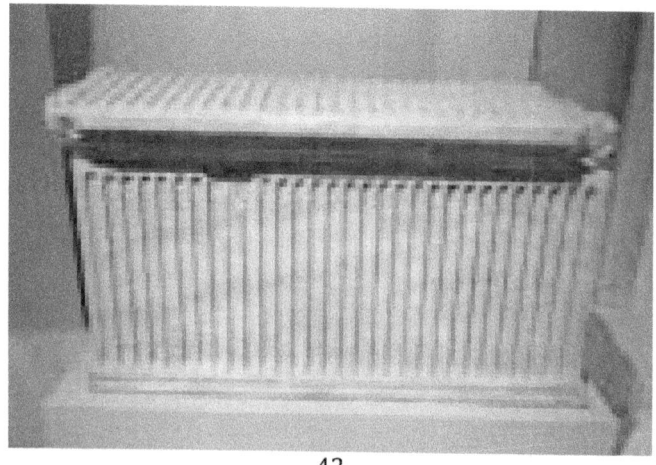

Ryan and Chang find the first evidence of life on mars.

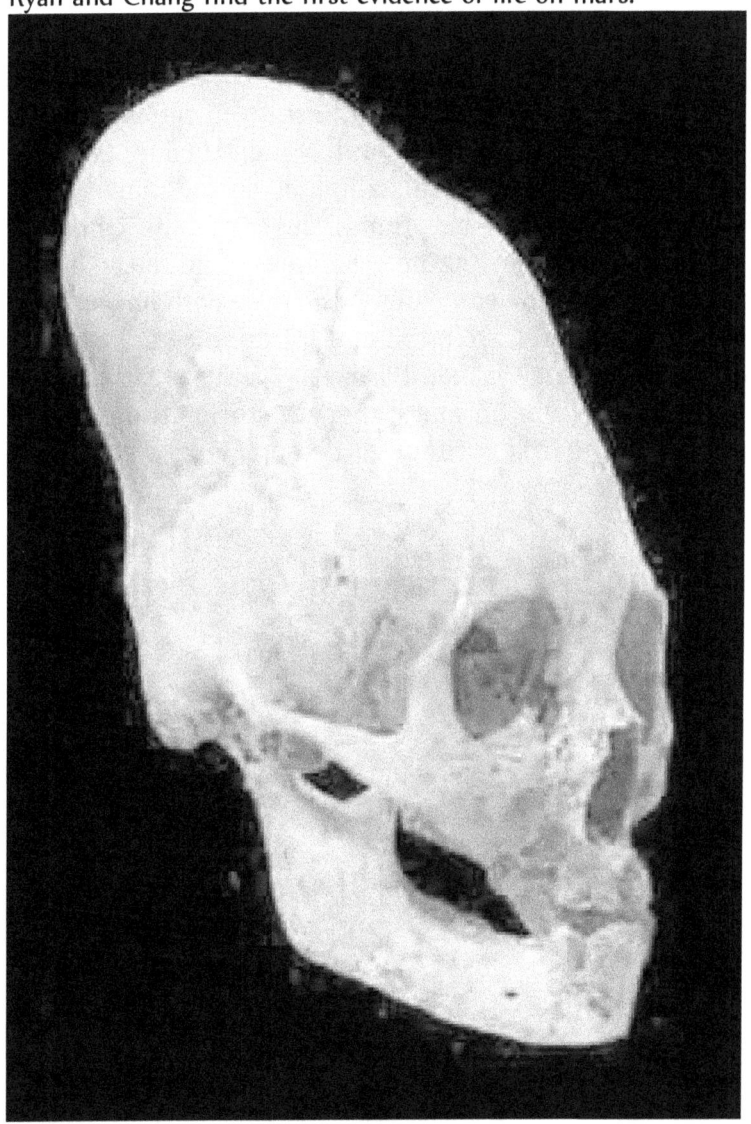

They photograph the corridor, the tomb and the skull and decide to head back to base camp though much is left unexplored, especially the multi-story cavern. They programmed Dixie GPS to explore the cavern and return the data remotely for further exploration by the crew.

CHAPTER VII

The space cart had unwound a hose from the greenhouse to the underground river of ice melt inside the cave. Bluford busied himself installing a cut-off valve and a battery operated solar pump just outside the cave entrance. He connected the greenhouse end of the hose to the valve and Dante came out of the cave with her hose.

"Everything set up in the underground river? How are you coming along?" asked Bluford, "We're starting up the first water system on Mars; that's historic, Anna. It's also going to be the first outdoor garden on Mars to be watered on the surface.

Bluford turns on the first Martian water system.

Courtesy of NASA website.

Bluford pressed down on the handle and saw water inflating the hose. For the first time, water was being directed by man unto the surface of arid Mars.

"The possibilities seem endless now," said Anna, overjoyed with the success of their work.

THE HOSE BRINGING WATER FROM THE ICE CAVES TO BASE

Water flows on the surface of Mars for the first time in 6,000 years. The news electrifies the world.

When Dante and Bluford returned to base, Marta was planting seeds and hardy moss in the saturated ground outside the greenhouse. "You guys are miracle workers. Water on Mars!"

"Have you heard from Ryan and Chang?" asked Dante.

"Their last communication was about digging into what they thought was a lava tube.   If they entered it, communication would be cut off.

They've been gone five hours now,"

Dante and Bluford continued to make finer adjustments to the water flow in various buildings at the base. They filled the 3-D printers' tanks with Martian soil, water and hardening compounds to make building blocks for further construction.

3-D printer building a house on Mars.

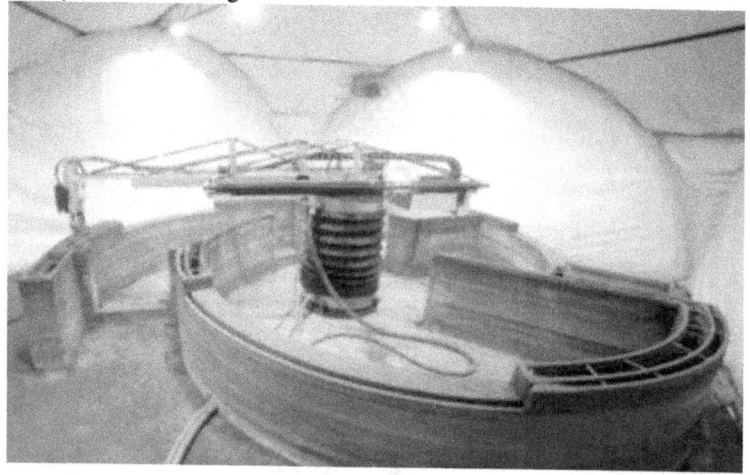

Future astronauts will have a larger base and will be able to stay even longer on Mars. 3-D printers can be programmed from Earth, but work even faster with nuclear power on site. They can make any tool or item needed from musical instruments to plates and kitchen utensils. They are also able to treat on-site trauma and wounds by replicating layers of skin and tissue in an emergency. In the future 3-D surgical robots will be able to operate on astronauts who break legs or other body parts. They will be able to print prostheses, custom-made for the individual astronaut.

Long term, the dream is to be able to print organs on demand with medical 3-D printers.

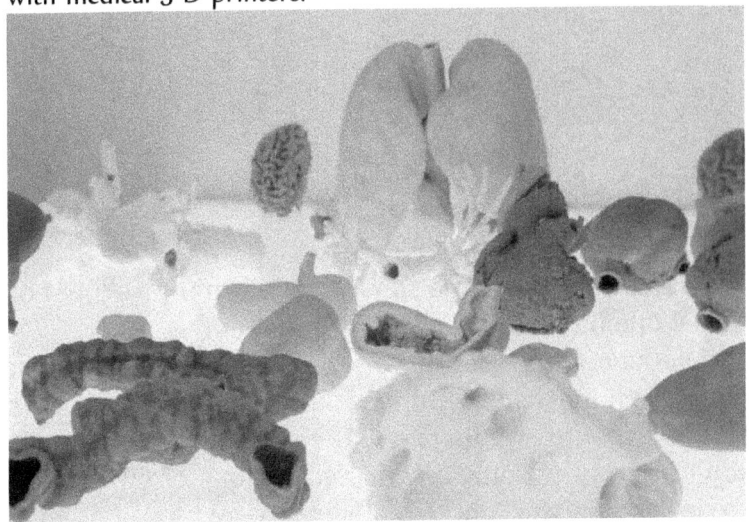

As soon as Ryan and Chang exited the underground room they reported finding the skull, the rooms and underground cavern. "Now we have an idea what a Martian looks like. We only found one skull in an ossuary. We'll have to come back later and resume the search," said Ryan.

"We now have a permanent source of running water on Mars. We are planting mosses, trees and bushes resistant to ultraviolet rays and extreme cold. We are also laying out more solar arrays and mirrors to try and warm up our area," said Bluford.

"With these stackable solar arrays I think we'll get out at least one hundred today."

"We have only been here for five days and look what we've accomplished. I do wonder if there are any living Martians feeling we invaded their space. Chang and I didn't see any writing, art, or decorations of any kind on the ossuary. I'm not even sure there are any living Martians. I wonder what happened?" Ryan was amazed at the progress they had made in only five days. The base was growing in size daily.

When Ryan and Chang arrived with the all-terrain vehicle, Bluford had already placed the hose into a valve cut-off, buried it and now they had control of the water flow at the base. "Great job, Jim," said Ryan.

"How does it feel to be the first man in history to bring flowing water to the surface of Mars?"

Bluford releases water from the ice cave to water ultraviolet-resistant plants in the greenhouse and outside.

CHAPTER VIII

"NASA reported that the danger of a nuclear Armageddon had passed on Earth and that every nation in the world was mesmerized by the televised discovery of water on Mars and Ryan and Chang's discovery of the rooms and skull at Diablo Canyon," said Commander Ryan. "There are many rooms still to be searched. Tomorrow four of us will go to Diablo Canyon and continue the search. It's a vast cavern and it was chosen by Martians as living quarters. Why, we don't know."

"The skull was very elongated and I've seen skulls in museums in Beijing like that when I was a child. A child's head is wrapped very early after birth and it forms like that. It was considered a mark of beauty and royalty in early dynasties," said Chang. "Well we'll know more tomorrow. The big question is what happened to the planet that forced Martians to spend their life underground."

"There was a high degree of magnetism in the area and it made me think of a scenario that could cause a mass extinction and change in the atmosphere — that would be a polar inversion, a flip of the poles if you will. It would change a habitable planet into an uninhabitable planet in an instant. Or maybe a massive comet or meteor hit Mars and caused a mass extinction similar to the one that killed off the dinosaurs on Earth. These are scenarios we have to consider," said Ryan.

"I wouldn't rule out a nuclear holocaust or climate change being the culprit," said Marta. "I kind of lean toward a climate change scenario. We now know Mars was once habitable because of the rooms and skull."

Did asteroids kill off all life on Mars or was it climate change, a nuclear war, the poles flipping or some other mass extinction? The astronauts wanted to know.

On the seventh day, Bluford, Chang, Ryan and Marta entered the ossuary room, saw the skull and started their search of the lower rooms.

The rooms were empty of art, writing or any kind of decorations. They gathered together at the bottom near a huge lake and entered a dark opening fifty yards ahead. They gasped as they entered a huge basalt cavern and saw four square columns and a cavern stacked with smaller columns and metal spheres like diving bells. A feathery veil-like material hung overhead. This cavern was developed and built by a highly advanced, intelligent community. Marta opened the bell and stepped inside the instrument-laden panel. Strange markings and what appeared to be writing labeled the panel's instruments. "I wonder what this bell was used for. Is it being used for the lake outside or for some other purpose?"

"It could be a capsule of some sort being dropped by a parachute, but with so many instruments it must fly," said Ryan.

"What is this disc on the side of the wall. It seems to have writing on it. I'm going to take a picture and send it to NASA. Do any of you recognize the script. It's written in a code of some sort," said Bluford.

"It seems to have been of some importance as it is held up by a special support, almost as if it were venerated," said Chang. "It seems like some sort of Rosetta stone. If only we could break the the code." He photographed both sides of the disc and would send it back to NASA in the hope that codebreakers would make sense of it.

They left the large room and entered a passageway. In the distance they could hear the sound of roaring water which got louder as they proceeded forward. "Wow," said Ryan. "Look at what the roaring water did here, it ate through what looks like basalt. I think we've gone as far

as we can go today. Dynamic forces are melting the ice in the soil and are creating a wonderland below," said Ryan. The group stared at the wondrous scene before them and pondered how long the channel of water flowed before settling in an underground lake of sorts.

They returned to base camp and downloaded all the video and photographs they had taken to NASA. The world back home was captivated by the discoveries *Courage One* was making and, after the tremendous destruction back home, plans for an international exploration of Mars was underway. The UN was making progress with its effort to denuclearize the entire world after the *war to end all wars.*

The 3-D printers had been programmed from day one to build greenhouses and outbuildings to be used for various functions in the future. Computerized planters were seeding the soil with hardy plants that would grow on Mars. Oxygen producing extremophile bacteria were being released in the hope they would propagate and oxygenate the atmosphere after many years. In the greenhouse, more seedlings were being nursed for planting. Now that water was available, drip hoses released water inside and outside the greenhouses. Mirrors were set up at intervals to magnify the sun's warmth on the base camp to help the plants grow faster. Fans gathered the oxygen released by the plants through photosynthesis and released it into the atmosphere.

Ryan thought about the skull they had discovered and knew they would have to go back to the cavern and explore it further. They were getting close to discovering something — something important.

NASA tanks store oxygen from a nuclear generator and from plants grown in the greenhouse. It is released into the atmosphere on Mars, which has only one percent oxygen on the surface. The plan is to make Mars breathable in fifty years.

Ryan could feel the building excitement. To be the first humans from Earth to arrive on Mars could only be surpassed by being the first humans since the dawn of humankind to interact with extra terrestrial beings.

The next day Ryan, Chang and Bluford returned to Diablo Canyon and entered the cavern. They searched each room they had missed and finally at the base they went down steps and couldn't believe their eyes.

Before them was a room with a wooden chest and a series of other rooms. "People are living here. I just can't believe it. How did they get here; who are they? These furnishing are human size. That looks like a kitchen ahead and those are platters for eating," said Bluford. "I wonder what kind of food they eat here on Mars?" Bluford, Ryan and Dante opened the the cabinets and pulled out draws but found nothing. "It's like an exhibition room or museum or like an apartment a realtor would show in an *open house*," said Dante.

Ryan walked ahead through a series of passageways and came upon a carpeted room with a table and a light overhead that was lit.

"It's as if someone just got up and left, wait until NASA hears about this. He videotaped the rooms and everything in them and then took stills of all the pictures which depicted scenes from nature and environments you would see on Earth: grassy knolls, trees, deserts, pyramids, etc.; but devoid of human life. He went to another picture and saw hyroglyphics and realized that there was a pharaoh pictured and other Egyptian figures. "There's a theme running through these pictures. Look, here's a pharaoh and his subjects. How could they know about Egypt?

"It looks like some kind of meeting among kings being mediated by a child. There are lots of figures. Is that the Sun God Ra? It looks like the guy is presenting a woman to a smaller king or pharaoh. What kind of exchange took place between between Egyptians and Martians," asked Bluford?

They went further into the apartment until they came to a room that seemed filled with sand, with a small opening near what once was a doorway. After clearing away the sand, they entered the chamber and saw what looked like Egyptian hiroglyphics etched on the far wall.

They were dumbstruck — the hiroglyphics depicted helicopters, airplanes and what appeared to be a car, tank and submarine. "Were Martians actually humans?" asked Chang. They continued on and went through a corridor. Up ahead they could hear dripping water. When they pointed their 500-watt lanterns, they were stunned to see a huge cavern before them.

A 250 foot stalagtite had calcified over millions of years and water was dripping down it, adding to its bulk. A pool of blue water surrounded the base and poured into another corridor. "There are lights coming from five passageways down there but I don't know how we can get down there. I think we have to backtrack, look for another entrance or return to base and try again another day. We're falling behind on some of the work we have to do at base. We'll send the video we have back to NASA and hear what they think we should do," said Ryan. They all agreed to head back to base.

Chang said, "I think we should lower Dixie GPS and let him explore the passageways and get video feed for us.."

"Great idea," said Bluford and they proceeded to program Dixie for twenty-four hours of reconnaisance with live video to begin in an hour. He was to return to the exact spot to be retrieve by the crew. They lowered him 250 feet and to initiate movement threw a yellow ball for him to retrieve. It was GPS locator he would carry around for the entire trip.

The crew could view everything Dixie saw and direct his movements.

CHAPTER IX

Bluford, Chang and Ryan return to base camp and buildings that were created by 3-D printers in seven days.

As soon as Bluford, Chang and Ryan returned to base camp, they downloaded all their video and photographs. Back on Earth, news of the *Courage One* crew's findings were setting rating records all over the world. Dixie's GPS video footage was keeping people up at nights. When Dixie entered a vast underground cavern everyone viewing the video stared spellbound at their screens as they viewed what looked to be a flying saucer coming in for a landing. Dante slowed Dixie's movement between two boulders so he would not be seen by the Martians. People on Earth were anxiously waiting to view Martians for the first time in history. A metallic ladder slowly emanated from the saucer and gently touched the surface.

Dixie was programmed to move closer to the flying saucer as the doors opened. The crew of *Courage One* couldn't believe their eyes when they saw dozens of figures emerging from the saucer and walking toward a small city.

"What is going on here? They are humans just like us. How can that be? They must be breathing carbon dioxide like we breathe oxygen," said Ryan.

"And that futuristic city is mind boggling. I think we are witnessing an advanced civilization that has been living underground for thousands of years," said Bluford. "Marta, have Dixie get closer so we can see their faces." Ryan took out binoculars for a close-up.

"That means those flying saucers sightings on Earth were for real and we kept debunking them," said Chang. "Look how happy the people seem. It's as if they are are strolling down Fifth Avenue. You have to admit their architecture is beautiful. But they can't seem to adjust to

surface radiation. How can such an advanced society be unable to live on the surface? Could they have arrived on Earth millions of years ago? What language do they speak? Should we make contact with them? All this video is being aired by NASA and is being televised all over the world. Who knew a computerized dog would reveal contact with Martians?"

"Program Dixie to focus on the west, Marta," said Ryan.

"Look at the public transportation they have and the apartment buildings and all the greeenery. That looks like a power plant in the distance. We can learn so much from them. I hope NASA says try and make contact with them. What made this cavern so huge, was it manmade? So many questions," said Ryan. Why have they shown no interest in contacting us?"

"Maybe, they don't know we are here," said Bluford.

"I think they've been watching us since we landed," said Ryan.

"Marta, program Dixie to enter the city, especially near what looks to be a huge greenhouse. I don't know if you know it but we are the most highly rated TV show all over the world. People are glued to their TV sets. It's a good thing because it allows clean-up crews on Earth to do their jobs. Certain areas of America have been devastated," said Ryan. "We'll get back on our feet as we always have," Ryan continued, echoing his days at the Air Force Academy.

As they watched, Dixie made his way toward the futuristic city and the greenhouse.

The crew of *Courage One* stood in amazement as Dixie wandered into the futuristic city and marveled at the multi-colored flying drones with humans inside. The city sprawled before them into the distance.

"This is incredible. How are they getting a light source to create so much greenery? Are they using radiation and battery storage on a grand scale? Is it possible they are not breathing carbon dioxide but oxygen? Can we breathe oxygen and take off these bulky suits?" asked Ryan.

"I don't think I would do it until we enter the area Dixie GPS is in," said Bluford.

Dixie walked into the beautiful city before him and the crew of *Courage One* marveled at what they were seeing. A civilization so modern and futuristic, it seemed as if they had solved every problem plaguing Earth. Greenery was everywhere. Dixie walked into what look to be a huge aircraft hangar and saw a woman working on what appeared to be a flying saucer. One revelation after another revealed a city so advanced it boggled the mind.

"I think it is time Dixie Two joined her mother, Dixie, because her audio/video is better. The fact that she's a lap dog, that she's cute and adorable and that she will make people want to hold her, makes her our secret weapon. Especially helpful as there are only five of us." said Ryan.

Dixie Two walked into the city toward the greenhouse at dusk.

Dixie Two ran into a hangar and took video of a woman working on what appeared to be a flying saucer with the camera embedded in her collar. Then she sauntered into a huge enclosed city that occupied miles of surburban space replete with a river running through it.

A NASA rendering depicting a futuristic city on Mars.

The crew of *Courage One* waited until midnight before they entered the city. There were just a few stragglers walking outside the the park near the greenhouse. Ryan told Marta and Chang to return to the base.

"We'll return in six hours. If not, wait a day. If we dont return, begin to make plans to return to Earth. I believe we can make contact with these people and learn their story and learn about their extraordinary technology."

"Don't you think you are taking an extraordinary risk? This was not on the NASA "to-do" list," said Chang.

"Nothing ventured, nothing learned. These people may be able to help us in some way," said Ryan.

"We never expected to come across a situation like this; it may be our only chance to come in contact with alien life even though they look like us," said Ryan.

"O.K., you're the commander," said Chang. They hugged those remaining and set out to return to base.

Ryan, Dante and Bluford entered the entrance to the dome. It opened automatically and, as they entered, a man and a woman happily walked up to them and welcomed them to their Martian city, Pacia. They spoke perfect English. "We've been waiting to meet you and are so glad you are here. You can take off those bulky suits and join us for refreshments." They were led to a conference room and smiling aides gave them fresh clothes and led them to seats in the spacious room.

The three crew members were amazed when tea and coffee were offered. The leader introduced himself as Chanso and his wife, Altea. "You must be weary from your courageous journey to our planet. I've been to Earth many times and know of your long journey. I know your first question must be: "Why do we live underground and why have we not contacted you before? To answer the first question. Six thousand years ago we had a nuclear war. Our planet was destroyed and our population was reduced by ninety percent. Because of the intense radiation, the only way to survive was to live underground. It took us 6,000 years to achieve what we have today. We were an advanced society then. Some chose to leave and, when we arrived in Egypt, we blended in among the people and helped them advance. We returned from Egypt with a new understanding of building massive structures underground. We learn things from you, too, and try to impart our wisdom to Earth by blending in as professors in your universities. We tried our best to stop World War I and World War ll. Once you developed the atomic bomb, we knew where you were headed was only a matter of time and we were not surprised at the catastophe you are suffering now. Because we have suffered catastrophe ourselves, we have said never again. As you can see, we are still suffering in that we cannot live on the surface because we had total war. On Earth you still have a chance to redeem yourself because of limited nuclear strikes," said Chanso.

All our tables are round and everyone is listened to.

"How do you resolve conflict and opposing views?" asked Ryan.

"We work at consensus; we have a UN that works. We are not big on titles. We believe in the Golden Rule and we believe it is wiser to listen than talk. Of course, our population is smaller. Most of all, we remember our Holocaust. We have outlawed nuclear weapons, but maintain a fleet of laser flying saucers for self defense, and so far we have remained a peaceful society. Our slowest saucer averages 4,280 miles per hour while our fastest goes over 17,000 miles per hour."

"You see, we are the human race of the future. We time traveled to Mars and have been here for thousands of years. When we first arrived here, we had to make it habitable and we did. For thousands of years we had an advanced civilization and made technological advances in artificial intelligence, computers, spacecraft and medicine. Somehow we lost control of our AI and robots began to duplicate themselves and saw us as the enemy. One of our engineers went rogue and thought he could create his own kingdom of robots and destroy humanity. For years tensions escalated and the robots replicated themselves and started to develop advanced weapons. The engineer declared himself president and many people died in a nuclear holocaust. We only returned to Earth when our planet became uninhabitable and learned from the Egyptians how to build great fortresses underground. Then we returned to Mars and built all you see before you.

A soldier in a robotic army created by artificial intelligence.

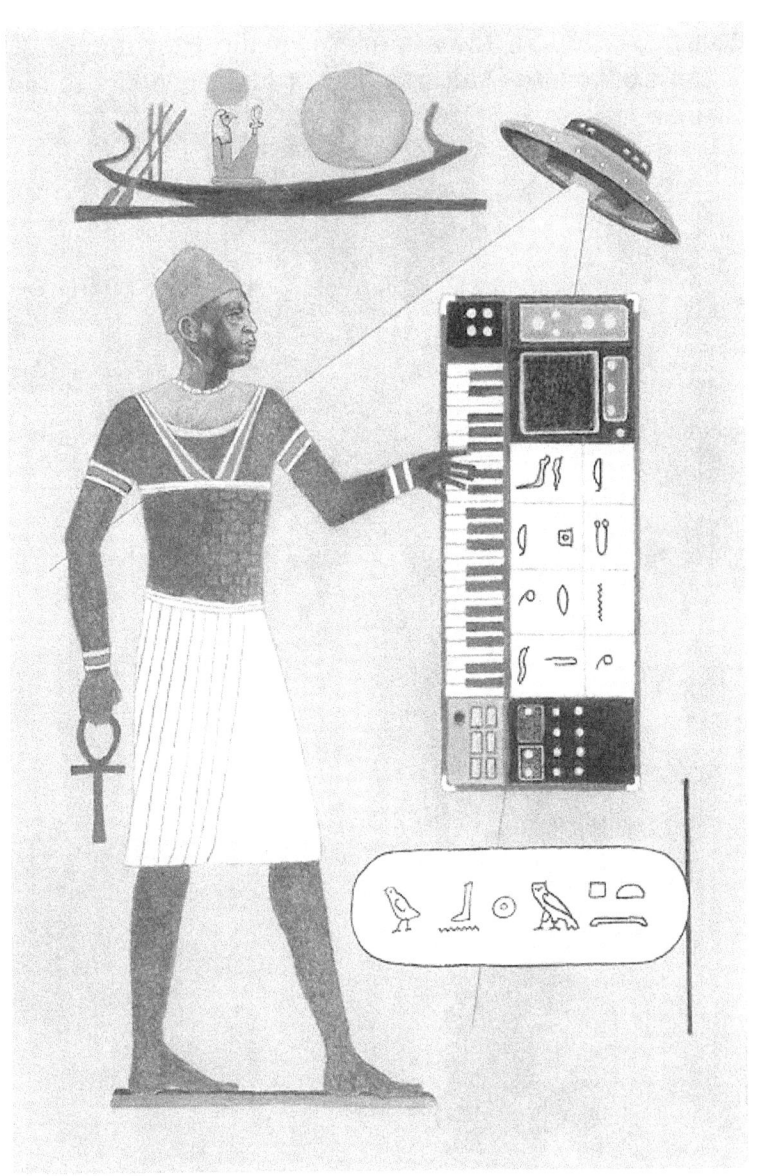

We introduced music, medicine and art, and learned building techniques that allowed us to build cities underground. We tutored pharaohs in geometry and academics and helped them build canals and terraced gardens. They were able to defeat many of their enemies because we taught them modern medical techniques. It was an exchange of cultures that brought benefits to both cultures.

A flying saucer seen over Passaic County, New Jersey, in 1952.

The numerous sightings you have seen on Earth were not hallucinations or fabrications but attempts to understand Earth better. We did have one notable accident at Roswell in New Mexico.

But our scientists were able to convince people a weather balloon failed.

Martians have ten varieties of flying saucers.

CHAPTER X

"But with all this technology, why don't you terraform the surface and make it habitable?" asked Ryan.

"We tried a number of times and failed, but now we know Earth has some plants and organisms that can survive in extreme conditions so we'll double-up our efforts to terraform since we have seen how you succeeded. That are other problems we must overcome: ultraviolet radiation, freezing temperatures and the need for gravity to name a few," said Chanso.

NASA's plan for terraforming the martian surface.

"We have a number of ideas we want to try in the future; getting water to the surface from the ice cave has been our greatest accomplishment so far. We also have oxygen being generated aboard our spaceship and released into the atmospere." said Bluford. "We are hoping the extremophile grasses and trees we have planted will increase the oxygen level on Mars from one percent to twenty-one percent in fifty years or sooner.

"We're also trying to heat up the atmosphere to block the ultraviolet rays bombarding Mars by using mirrors and a variety of other means," said Ryan. "By utilizing hydrothermal vents we can heat Mars."

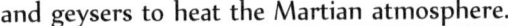
Vents clogged for millions of years are re-bored, releasing steam and geysers to heat the Martian atmosphere.

"We have some plans to pump greenhouse gases and turn the underground dry ice into an energy source and steam to heat the the planet. There are thousands of ideas people from Earth have suggested and scientists want to try," said Dante.

"And many we have never thought of. We remain sceptical because all our prior efforts have failed with great loss of life whenever we became obsessed with making a heaven on Earth underground. You have to understand we've been living with a nuclear holocaust for over 6,000 years," said Altea. "The surface was a living hell for thousands of years. The atmosphere was poisoned with radiation, devastating winds, dust storms and finally freezing temperatures. Millions of people were killed and millions died within a year of cancer, radiation, leukemia and blood poisoning. I'm talking about a horrible, agonizing death no one deserves.

Mars became a barren wasteland after a nuclear war.

Books recount the painful tale of people running for the lava tubes, where supplies had been stored when fears of a nuclear war led to prudent preparation for a nuclear war. Pandemonium and panic ruled.

Workers prepare the tunnels for survival in a nuclear war.

They took a lava tube like this and worked on it to begin the process of turning it into a storage cavern that could be accessed from above.

All order broke down and it was every man, women and child for themselves. The children suffered the most, being separated from their parents and guardians. Never in Martian history did such destruction occcur. We were a planet on fire, every living thing on the surface was obliterated within seconds.

This martian blast was multiplied thousands of times over, destroying everything within a two hundred mile radius. Outside that zone people died of cancers and pulmonary diseases and many other ailments within days. The only survivors were those who fled to the lava tubes and brought with them their pets, plants, seeds and possessions. This event occurred 6,000 years ago on Mars.

We offered incentives for the adults who survived to have children. Every ten years or so we would connect to more survivors who had sought shelter in the lava tubes; many were in emaciated condition, had no access to food and mininmal water. We broke through many lava tubes looking for survivors and found thousands. Slowly we began to build the city, increase agricultural growth using aquaponics and gatherred our finest architects, engineers, scientists, city planners, designers, physicians, educators, teachers, clergy, geologists, homebuilders and tunnel experts to create the city you see before you.

Rendering courtesy of NASA website.

After seventy-five days on Mars, the *Courage One* crew have explored the Martian City and helped terraform the city with solar farms, infrared-resistant plants and oxygen producing bacteria and extremophiles.

Courtesy of NASA website.

CHAPTER XI

"The thing we haven't talked about, and I think you should know, is why a nuclear war started in the first place. A local province had a popular leader who believed in income distribution, social welfare and stopping ownership of private property and businesses. Everything would be owned by the people. At first he was extremely popular, legalizing opioieds, marajuana and other drugs and opening schools to everyone regardless of intellectual abilities. He distributed the state's wealth equally among all the people. Intellectuals and business owners were sent to re-education camps. The common people elected him and he established a local militia that grew into a substantial army. Opposition to him disappeared or died from assasination.

Emboldened by his success and popularity and longevity in office he decided he wanted to spread his democratic ideals to neighboring provinces until vast sections of the planet were under his dominion. Any opposition to his policies of power to the people were harshly dealt with through assasination, disappearances and jailings. In the West he was seen as a tyrant and opposition to his policies were aided with armament, financial aid and local battles for control. He vowed to punish the West for its meritocracy and refusal to distribute its wealth equally among it citizens. In the beginning he called for socialism but he was a true believer in communism. He wanted to curtail the freedoms enjoyed by the West and called for the spread of communsm everywhere. An arms race ensued and localized skirmishes turned into battles for control of cities. The Central Committee ordered the development of more nuclear weapons. The West responded in kind. An accidental nuclear war started when solar flares were mistaken for incoming missiles and all hell broke loose. This all happened 6,000 years ago. All human progress on the surface was reduced to rubble and deadly radiation and that is why we are here today. The people of our planet have outlawed nuclear weapons ever since. The skull you found is the remains of the leader who decimated his planet and we call him *Death*," said Chanso.

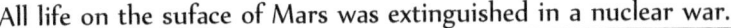

All life on the suface of Mars was extinguished in a nuclear war.

"And we seem to be repeating the same scenario on Earth," said Commander Ryan. "We've been here eighty-five days and have to leave next week. We've videotaped the interview with you and will send it immediately to our people on Earth. We've made great progress in the short time we've been here and know what works and what doesn't. We'll soon be making many trips to Mars and will speed up the oxygenation of your planet and raise the temperature and reduce the ultraviolet rays that cause so much havoc to the atmosphere. You are welcome to accompany us back to Earth if you like. I think of Mars like a sister planet and we can learn so much from you and what your people have accomplished over the centuries. I think the introduction of plant species and bacteria from Earth can benefit your planet immensely," said Ryan.

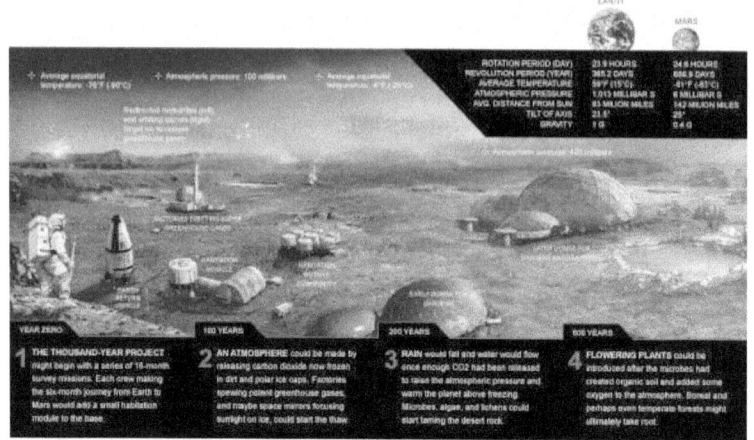

"We will introduce mobile, gas-emitting skyscrapers to heat up Mars. We will bring up water from the subsurface that is in the form of ice and create flowing rivers again on Mars. I think with a concentrated effort we can do this in a generation. With cooperation between our two planets and your advanced aerodynamic vessels we will explore the universe together and hopefully there will be war no more," said Ryan.

CHAPTER XII

Preparation for the Return to Earth

The crew of *Courage One* had been on Mars for eighty-six days and their exploits were the most-watched TV program on Earth. The crew programmed the 3-D printers to continue building a small city in their absence. Oxygen-emitting bacteria was growing on a large scale and miles of seeds that thrived in harsh Martian conditions were planted and irrigated by water brought up from the subsurface and released intermittently. Chanso and Ryan exchanged books, plans, samples, intellectual property, seeds, bacteria and everything that could benefit both societies in their quest for survival. They promised to visit each other regularly.

Chanso gave Ryan the complete blueprints to manufacturing flying saucers and Ryan gave him the entire plans for terraforming Mars.

Ryan gave Chanso a copy of the Bible, the works of Shakespeare and several volumes of NASA's work on terraforming Mars. He gave him samples of seeds and extremophile bacteria that emitted oxygen into the atmosphere and plans for building 3-D printers that used Martian surface resources as building material. Chanso came to the surface in a protective space suit and said goodbye to Commander Ryan and crew.

"I wanted to ask you Chanso, what kind of religious belief do your people practice?" asked Ryan.

"We believe in Jesus, the Redeemer. A man was born to a Martian mother two thousand years ago and lived among us. He performed many miracles. He was killed by unbelievers, but he rose from the dead after three days and many people believe he saved us from total destruction." Ryan said to himself. "He truly is the Son of God and rules the universe."

The crew made final arrangements for blast-off. They accomplished a lot in ninety days. Most of all, they brought hope to a suffering humanity and work towards terraforming Mars was well underway. The fact that Martians were like themselves led to many questions about evolution, religion, the history of the solar system and man's purpose in the universe.

"The underground world you created is simply amazing and protective of your people, in case of surface emergencies. Once we repair your surface with terraforming, your people will have room for expansion and exploration, and someday, together we'll explore the universe," said Ryan.

Martian and Earth space explorers explore the universe.

Ryan addressed the crew. "The ninety days we spent here will go down in history. The discoveries and work you've done here is groundbreaking and will set the course for further exploration of space. We have begun the terraforming of Mars and we've met extraordinarily friendly Martians.

Courage *One* blast-off from Mars, completing man's exploration of Mars.

Martians have shared their discoveries with us as we have with them. This exchange is only the beginning," said Commander Ryan.

Courage One returns to Earth to a hero's welcome.

Heritage Books by Tom Riley:

Andrew Horace Burke
A Man for All Seasons: The Incredible Story of an Orphan Train Rider
and Civil War Drummer Boy Who Grew Up to Become
the Governor of North Dakota

Happy Valley School: A History and Remembrance

Martian Odyssey

Orphan Train Riders: A Brief History of the Orphan Train Era (1854–1929)
with Entrance Records from the American Female Guardian
Society's Home for the Friendless in New York
Volume One

Orphan Train Riders: Entrance Records from the
American Female Guardian Society's Home
for the Friendless in New York
Volume Two

The Big Green Book: How the Environmental Decisions We Make in
These Turbulent Economic Times Will Effect America and the World

The History of Postal Services from 6,000 Years Ago to the Present:
The Earliest Known Writing Is Still Undecipherable

The Orphan Train to Destiny

The Stuyvesant Connection

We Deliver: A Chronicle of the Deeds Performed by the
Men and Women of the U.S. Postal Service